D1529597

BOOKS BY

THORNTON W. BURGESS

THE BEDTIME STORY-BOOKS

The Adventures of:

Reddy Fox	Johnny Chuck
Buster Bear	Danny Meadow Mouse
Peter Cottontail	Bobby Coon
Jimmy Skunk	Grandfather Frog

The Burgess Bird Book for Children
The Burgess Animal Book for Children
The Burgess Flower Book for Children
The Burgess Seashore Book for Children
The Wishing-Stone Stories
While the Story-Log Burns
On the Green Meadows
At the Smiling Pool
The Crooked Little Path
The Dear Old Briar-Patch

Old Mother West Wind	Mother West Wind "Why" Stories
Mother West Wind's Children	Mother West Wind "How" Stories
Mother West Wind's Animal Friends	Mother West Wind "When" Stories
Mother West Wind's Neighbors	Mother West Wind "Where" Stories

Happy Jack	Jerry Muskrat at Home
Mrs Peter Rabbit	Longlegs the Heron
Bowser the Hound	Lightfoot the Deer
Old Granny Fox	Blacky the Crow
Billy Mink	Whitefoot the Woodmouse
Little Joe Otter	Buster Bear's Twins

The Bedtime Story-Books

THE ADVENTURES OF
BOBBY COON

BY

THORNTON W. BURGESS

With Illustrations by

HARRISON CADY

BOSTON

LITTLE, BROWN AND COMPANY

1947

BURGESS TRADE QUADDIES MARK

PRINTED IN THE UNITED STATES OF AMERICA
Designed and Produced by Artists and Writers Guild, Inc.

CONTENTS

LIST OF ILLUSTRATIONS

Sometimes he would take a little walk for exercise. *See page* 2

CHAPTER I

Bobby Coon Has a Bad Dream

Some dreams are good and some are bad;
  Some dreams are light and airy;
Some dreams I think are woven by
  The worst kind of a fairy.

Dreams are such queer things, so very real when all the time they are unreal, that sometimes I think they must be the work of fairies—happy dreams the work of good fairies and bad dreams the work of bad fairies. I guess you've had both kinds. I know I have many times. However, Bobby Coon says that fairies have nothing to do with dreams. Bobby ought to know, for he spends most of the winter asleep, and it is only when you are asleep that you have real dreams.

Bobby had kept awake as long as there was anything to eat, but when Jack Frost froze everything hard, and rough Brother North Wind brought the storm-clouds that covered the Green Forest with snow, Bobby climbed into his warm bed inside the big hollow chestnut tree which he called his, curled up comfortably, and went to sleep. He didn't care a hair of his ringed tail how cold it was or how Brother North Wind howled and shrieked and blustered. He was so fat that it made him wheeze and puff whenever he tried to hurry during the last few days he was abroad, and this fat helped to keep him warm while he slept, and also kept him from waking from hunger.

Bobby didn't sleep right straight through the winter as does Johnny Chuck. Once in a great while he would wake up, especially if the weather had turned rather warm. He would yawn a few times and then crawl up to his doorway and peep out to see how things were looking outside. Sometimes he would climb down from his home and take a little walk for exercise. But he never went far, and soon returned for another long nap.

As it began to get towards the end of winter his naps were shorter. He was no longer fat. In fact, his stomach complained a great deal of being empty. Perhaps you know what it is like to have a stomach complain that way. It is very disturbing. It gave Bobby no peace while he was awake, and when he was asleep it gave him bad dreams. Bobby knew very well that no fairies had anything to do with those dreams; they came from a bothersome, empty, complaining stomach and nothing else.

One day Bobby had the worst dream of all. He had prowled around a little the night before but had found nothing wherewith to satisfy his bothersome stomach. So he had gone back to bed very much out of sorts and almost as soon as he was asleep he had begun to dream. At first the dreams were not so very bad, though bad enough. They were mostly of delicious things to eat which always disappeared just as he was about to taste them. They made him grunt funny little grunts and snarl funny little impatient snarls in his sleep, you know.

But at last he began to have a really, truly, bad dream. It was one of the worst dreams Bobby had ever had. He dreamed that he was walking through the Green Forest, minding his own affairs, when he met a great giant. Being afraid of the great giant, he ran with all his might and hid in a hollow log. No sooner was he inside that hollow log than up came the great giant and began to beat on that hollow log with a great club. Every blow made a terrible noise inside that hollow log. It was like being inside a drum with someone beating it. It filled Bobby's ears with a dreadful roaring. It made his head ache as if it would split. It sent cold shivers all over him. It filled him with dreadful fear and despair. Yes, indeed, it was a bad dream, a very, very bad dream!

CHAPTER II

Bobby Bites His Own Tail

"Oh tell me, someone, if you will
Am I awake or dreaming still?"

So cried Bobby Coon to no one in particular, because no one was there to hear him. Bobby was in a dreadful state of mind. He couldn't tell for the life of him whether he was awake, or asleep and dreaming, and I cannot think of a much worse state of mind than that, can you?

There was that dreadful dream Bobby had had, the dream of the dreadful giant who had chased him into a hollow log and then beat on that log with a great club, frightening Bobby almost to death, filling his ears with a terrible roaring sound that made his head ache, and sending cold shivers all over him. Bobby was trying to make up his mind to rush out of that hollow log in spite of the dreadful giant, all in his dream you know, when suddenly his eyes flew open and there he was safe in his bed in the hollow chestnut tree which he called his own.

5

Bobby Coon crouched down and started to whimper. *See page 23*

Bobby gave a happy little sigh of relief, it seemed so good to find that dreadful experience only a dream. "Phew!" he exclaimed. "That was a bad, bad dream!" And then right on top of that he gave a little squeal of fear. There was that awful pounding again! Was he still dreaming? Was he awake? For the life of him Bobby couldn't tell. There was that same dreadful pounding he had heard in the hollow log, but he wasn't in the hollow log; he was safe at home in his own warm bed. Had he somehow reached home without knowing it, in the strange way that things are done in dreams, and had the dreadful giant followed him? That must be it. It must be that he was still dreaming. He wished that he would wake up.

Bobby closed his eyes as tightly as he knew how for a few minutes. Pound, pound, pound, sounded the dreadful blows. Then he opened his eyes. Surely this was his hollow tree, and certainly he felt very much awake. There was the sunlight peeping in at his doorway high overhead. Yet still those dreadful blows sounded—pound, pound, pound. His head ached still, harder than ever. And with every blow he jumped, and a cold shiver ran over him from the roots of his tail to the tip of his nose.

Never in all his life had Bobby known such a mixed-up feeling. "Is this I, or isn't it I?" he whimpered. "Am I dreaming and think I'm awake, or am I awake and still dreaming? I know what I'll do; I'll bite my tail, and if I feel it I'll know that I must be awake."

So Bobby took the tip of his tail in his mouth and bit it gently. Then he wondered if he really did feel it or just seemed to. So he bit it again, and this time he bit harder.

"Ouch!" cried Bobby. "That hurt. I must be awake. I'm sure I'm awake. But if I'm awake, what dreadful thing is happening? Is there a real giant pounding on my tree?"

Then Bobby noticed something else. With every blow his house seemed to tremble. At first he thought he imagined it, but when he put his hands against the wall, he felt it tremble. It gave him a horrid sinking feeling inside. He was sure now that he was awake, very much awake. He was sure, too, that something dreadful was happening to his hollow tree, and he couldn't imagine what it could be. And what is more, he was afraid to climb up to his doorway and look out to see.

CHAPTER III

Bobby's Dreadful Fright

Poor, poor Bobby Coon. Now he was sure that he was really and truly awake, he almost wished that he hadn't tried to find out. It would have been some little comfort to have been able to keep his first feeling that maybe it was all a bad dream. But now that he knew positively he was awake, he knew that this terrible pounding, which at first had been part of that bad dream, was also real. The truth is, he could no longer doubt that something terrible was happening to his house, the big hollow chestnut tree he had lived in so long.

With every blow, and the blows followed each other so fast that he couldn't count them, the big tree trembled, and Bobby trembled with it. What could it mean? What could be going on outside? He wanted to climb up to his doorway and look out, but somehow he didn't dare to. He was afraid of what he might see. Yes, Sir, Bobby Coon was afraid to climb up to his doorway and look out for fear he might see something that would frighten him more than he was already frightened, though how he could possibly have been any more frightened I don't know. Yet all the time it didn't seem to him that he could stay where he was another minute. No, Sir, it didn't. He was too frightened to go and too frightened to stay. Now can you think of anything worse than that?

The tree trembled more and more, and by and by it began to do more than tremble; with a dreadful, a very dreadful sinking of his heart, Bobby felt his house begin to sway, that is, move a little from side to side. A new fear drove everything else out of his head—the fear that his house might be going to fall! He couldn't believe that this could be true, yet he had the feeling that it was so. He couldn't get rid of it. He had lived in that house a long, long time and never in all that long, long time had he once had such a feeling as now possessed him. Many a time had rough Brother North Wind used all his strength against that big chestnut tree. Sometimes he had made it tremble ever so little, but that was all, and Bobby, curled up in his snug bed, had laughed at rough Brother North Wind. He just couldn't imagine anything happening to his tree.

But something *was* happening now. There wasn't the smallest doubt about it. The great old tree shivered and shook with every blow. At last Bobby could stand it no longer. He just *had* to know what was happening, and what it all meant. With his teeth chattering with fright, he crawled up to his doorway and looked down. Badly frightened as he was, what he saw frightened him still more. It frightened him so that he let go his hold and tumbled down to his bed. Of course that didn't hurt him, because it was soft, and in a minute he was scrambling up to his doorway again.

"What shall I do? What *can* I do?" whimpered Bobby Coon as he looked down with frightened eyes. "I can't run and I can't stay. What can I do? What can I do?"

Bobby Coon was horribly frightened. There was no doubt about it, he was horribly frightened. Have you guessed what it was that he saw? Well, it was Farmer Brown and Farmer Brown's boy chopping down the big chestnut tree which had been Bobby's home for so long. And looking on was Bowser the Hound.

CHAPTER IV

Bowser Finds Someone at Home

Now that Bobby Coon knew what it was that had frightened him so, he felt no better than before. In fact, he felt worse. Before, he had imagined all sorts of dreadful things, but nothing that he had imagined was as bad as what he now knew to be a fact. His house, the big hollow chestnut tree in which he had lived so long and in which he had gone to sleep so happily at the beginning of winter, was being cut down by Farmer Brown's boy and Farmer Brown himself, and Bowser the Hound was looking on. There was no other tree near enough to jump to. The only way out was down right where those keen axes were at work and where Bowser sat watching. What chance was there for him? None. Not the least chance in the world. At least, that is the way Bobby felt about it. That was because he didn't know Farmer Brown and Farmer Brown's boy.

You see, all this time that Bobby Coon had been having

such a dreadful, such a very dreadful time, Farmer Brown and Farmer Brown's boy and Bowser the Hound had known nothing at all about it. Bobby Coon hadn't once entered the heads of any of them. None of them knew that the big chestnut tree was Bobby's home. If Farmer Brown's boy had known it, I suspect that he would have found some good excuse for not cutting it. But he didn't, and so he swung his axe with a will, for he wanted to show his father that he could do a man's work.

Why were they cutting down that big chestnut tree? Well, you see, that tree was practically dead, so Farmer Brown had decided that it could be of use in no way now save as wood for the fires at home. If it were cut down, the young trees springing up around it would have a better chance to grow. It would be better to cut it now than to allow it to stand, growing weaker all the time, until at last it should fall in some great storm and perhaps break down some of the young trees about it.

Now if Bobby Coon had known Farmer Brown and Farmer Brown's boy as Tommy Tit the Chickadee knew them, and as Happy Jack Squirrel knew them, and as some others knew them, he would have climbed right straight down that tree without the teeniest, weeniest bit of fear of them. He would have known that he was perfectly safe. But he didn't know them, and so he felt both helpless and hopeless, and this is a very dreadful feeling indeed.

For a little while he peeped out of his doorway, watching the keen axes and the flying yellow chips. Then he crept miserably back to bed to wait for the worst. He just didn't know what else to do. By and by there was a dreadful crack, and another and another. Farmer Brown shouted. So did Farmer Brown's boy. Bowser the Hound barked excitedly. Slowly the big tree began to lean over. Then it moved faster and faster, and Bobby Coon felt giddy and sick. He felt very sick indeed. Then, with a frightful crash, the tree struck the ground, and for a few minutes Bobby didn't know anything at all. No, sir, he didn't know a single thing. You see, when the tree hit the ground, Bobby was thrown against the side of his house so hard that all the wind was knocked from his body, and all his senses were knocked from his head. When after a little they returned to him, Bobby discovered that the tree had fallen in such a way that the hole which had been his doorway was partly closed. He was a prisoner in his own house.

He didn't mind this so much as you might expect. He began to hope ever so little. He began to hope that Farmer Brown and his boy wouldn't find that hollow and after a while they would go away. And then Bowser the Hound upset all hope. He came over to the fallen tree and began to sniff along the trunk. When he reached the partly closed hole which was Bobby's doorway, he began to whine and bark excitedly. He would stick his nose in as far as he could, sniff, then lift his head and bark. After that he would scratch frantically at the hole.

"Hello!" exclaimed Farmer Brown's boy, "Bowser has found someone at home! I wonder who it can be."

CHAPTER V

Bobby Coon Shows Fight

Who for his home doth bravely fight
Is doing what he knows is right.
A coward he, the world would say,
Should he turn tail and run away.

Bobby Coon couldn't run away if he wanted to. I suspect
that he would have run only too gladly if there had been the
least chance to. But there he was, a prisoner in his own
house. He couldn't get out if he wanted to, and he didn't
want to just then because he knew by the sound of Bowser
the Hound's deep sniffs at his doorway, followed by his
eager barks, that Bowser had discovered that he, Bobby,
was at home. He knew that Bowser couldn't get in, and so
he was very well content to stay where he was.

But presently Bobby heard the voice of Farmer Brown's
boy, and though Bobby didn't understand what Farmer
Brown's boy said, his heart sank away down to his toes just

the same. At least, that is the way it felt to Bobby. You see, he knew by the sound of that voice, even though he couldn't understand the words, that Farmer Brown's boy had understood Bowser, and now knew that there was someone at home in that hollow tree.

As to that Bobby was quite right. While Farmer Brown's boy couldn't understand what Bowser was saying as he whined and yelped, he did understand perfectly what Bowser meant.

"Who is it, Bowser, old fellow? Is it a squirrel, or Whitefoot the Wood Mouse, or that sly old scamp, Unc' Billy Possum?" asked Farmer Brown's boy.

"Bow, wow, wow!" replied Bowser, dancing about between sniffs at Bobby's doorway.

"I don't know what that means, but I'm going to find out, Bowser," laughed Farmer Brown's boy, picking up his axe.

"Bow, wow! Bow, wow, wow, wow!" replied Bowser, more excited than ever. First Farmer Brown's boy had Farmer Brown hold Bowser away from the opening. Then with his axe he thumped all along the hollow part of the tree, hoping that this would frighten whoever was inside so that he would try to run out. But Bobby couldn't get out because, as you know, his doorway was partly closed, and he wouldn't have even it he could; he felt safer right where he was. So Farmer Brown's boy thumped in vain. When he found that this was useless, he drove the keen edge of his axe in right at the edge of the hole which was Bobby's doorway. Farmer Brown joined with his axe, and in a few minutes they had slit out a long strip which reached clear to where Bobby was crouching and let the light pour in, so that he had to blink and for a minute or two had hard work to see at all.

Right away Bowser discovered him, and, growling savagely, tried to get at him. But the opening wasn't wide enough for Bowser to get more than his nose in, and this Bobby promptly seized in his sharp teeth.

"Yow-w-w! Oh-o-o! Let go! Let go!" yelled Bowser.

"Gr-r-r-r-r!" growled Bobby, and tried to sink his teeth deeper. Bowser yelled and howled and shook his head and pulled as hard as ever he could, so that at last Bobby had to let go. Farmer Brown's boy hurried up to look in. What he saw was a mouthful of sharp teeth snapping at him. Bobby Coon might have been very much afraid, but he didn't show it. No, sir, he didn't show it. What he did show was that he meant to fight for his life, liberty, and home. He was very fierce-looking, was Bobby Coon, as Farmer Brown's boy peeped in at him.

CHAPTER VI

Something Is Wrong with Bobby Coon

Farmer Brown's boy chuckled as he peered in at Bobby Coon, and watched Bobby show his teeth, and listened to his snarls and growls. It was very plain that Bobby intended to fight for his life. It might be an entirely helpless fight, but he would fight just the same.

"Bobby," said Farmer Brown's boy, "you certainly are a plucky little rascal. I know just what you think; you think that my father and I cut this tree down just to get you, and you think that we and Bowser the Hound are going to try to kill you. You are all wrong, Bobby, all wrong. If we had known that this tree was your house, we wouldn't have cut it down. No, sir, we wouldn't. And now that we have found out that it is, we are not going to harm so much as a hair of you. I'm going to cut this opening a little larger so that you can get out easily, and then I am going to hold on to Bowser and give you a chance to get away. I hope

Farmer Brown's boy waved good-by to Bobby Coon. *See page 45*

you know of some other hollow tree near here to which you can go. It's a shame, Bobby, that we didn't know about this. It certainly is, and I'm ever so sorry. Now you just quit your snarling and growling while I give you a chance to get out."

But Bobby continued to threaten to fight whomever came near. You see, he couldn't understand what Farmer Brown's boy said, which was too bad, because it would have lifted a great load from his mind. So he didn't have the least doubt that these were enemies and that they intended to kill him. He didn't believe he had the least chance in the world to escape, but he bravely intended to fight the very best he could, just the same. And this shows that Bobby possessed the right kind of a spirit. It shows that he wasn't a quitter. Furthermore, though no one knew it but himself, Bobby had been badly hurt when that tree fell. The fact is, one of Bobby's legs had been broken. Yet in spite of this, he meant to fight. Yes, sir, in spite of a broken leg, he had no intention of giving up until he had to.

Farmer Brown's boy swung his axe a few times and

split the opening in the hollow tree wider so that Bobby would have no trouble in getting out. All the time Bobby snapped and snarled and gritted his teeth. Then Farmer Brown's boy led Bowser the Hound off to one side and held him. Farmer Brown joined them, and then they waited. Bobby couldn't see them. It grew very still there in the Green Forest. Bobby didn't know just what to make of it. Could it be that he had frightened them away by his fierceness? After a while he began to think that this was so. He waited just as long as he could be patient and then poked his head out. No one was to be seen, for Farmer Brown and his boy and Bowser the Hound were hidden by a little clump of hemlock trees.

Slowly and painfully Bobby climbed out. That broken leg hurt dreadfully. It was one of his front legs, and of course he had to hold that paw up. That meant that he had to walk on three legs. This was bad enough, but when he started to climb a tree, he couldn't. With a broken leg, there would be no more climbing for Bobby Coon. It was useless for him to look for another hollow tree. All he could do was to look for a hollow log into which he could crawl. Poor Bobby Coon! What should he do? What *could* he do? For the first time his splendid courage deserted him. You see, he thought he was all alone there, and that no one saw him. So he just crouched right down there at the foot of the tree he had started to climb, and whimpered. He was frightened and very, very miserable, was Bobby Coon, and he was in great pain.

CHAPTER VII

Bobby Has a Strange Journey

It's funny how you'll often find
That trouble's mostly in your mind.

It's a fact. More than three fourths of the troubles that worry people are not real troubles at all. They are all in the mind. They are things that people are afraid are going to happen, and worry about until they are sure they will happen,—and then they do not happen at all. Very, very often things that seem bad turn out to be blessings. All of us do a great deal of worrying for nothing. I know I do. Bobby Coon did when he took his strange journey which I am going to tell you about.

Farmer Brown and Farmer Brown's boy and Bowser the Hound had watched Bobby crawl out of his ruined house and start off to seek a new home. Of course, they had seen right away that something was wrong with Bobby, for he walked on three legs and held the fourth one up.

"The poor little chap," murmured Farmer Brown's boy pityingly. "That leg must have been hurt when the tree fell. I hope it isn't badly hurt. We'll wait a few minutes and see what he does."

So they waited in their hiding place and watched Bobby. They saw him go to the foot of a tree as if to climb it. They saw him try and fail, because he couldn't climb with only three legs, and they saw him crouch down in a little whimpering heap because he thought he was all alone. It was then that Farmer Brown's boy was sure that Bobby's hurt was really serious.

"We can't let that little fellow go, to suffer and perhaps die," said Farmer Brown's boy, and ran forward while Farmer Brown held Bowser.

Bobby heard him coming and promptly faced about ready to fight bravely. When he got near enough, Farmer Brown's boy threw his coat over Bobby and then, in spite of Bobby's frantic struggles, gathered him up and wrapped the coat about him so that he could neither bite nor scratch. Bobby was quite helpless.

"I'm going to take him home, and when I've made him

quite comfortable, I'll come back," cried Farmer Brown's boy.

"All right," replied Farmer Brown, with a kindly twinkle in his eyes.

So Farmer Brown's boy started for home, carrying Bobby as gently as he could. Of course Bobby couldn't see where he was being taken, because that coat was over his head, and of course he hadn't understood a word that Farmer Brown's boy had said. But Bobby could imagine all sorts of dreadful things, and he did. He was sure that when this journey ended the very worst that could happen *would* happen. He was quite hopeless, was Bobby Coon. He kept still because he had to. There was nothing else to do.

All the time he wondered where he was being taken. He was sure that never again would he see the Green Forest. His broken leg pained him dreadfully, but fear of what would happen when this strange journey ended made him almost forget the pain. It was the first time in all his life that Bobby ever had journeyed anywhere save on his own four feet, and quite aside from his fear, it gave him a very queer feeling. He kept wishing it would end quickly, yet at the same time he didn't want it to end because of what he was sure would happen then.

So through the Green Forest, then through the Old Orchard, and finally across the barnyard to the barn Bobby Coon was carried. It was the strangest journey he ever had known and it was the most terrible, though it needn't have been if only he could have known the truth.

CHAPTER VIII

Farmer Brown's Boy Plays Doctor

No greater joy can one attain
Than helping ease another's pain.

Poor Bobby Coon! His broken leg pained him a great deal, of course. Broken legs and arms always do pain. They hurt dreadfully when they are broken, they hurt dreadfully after they are broken, and they hurt while they are mending. Among the little people of the Green Forest and the Green Meadows, a broken leg or arm is a great deal worse than it is with us humans. We know how to fix the break so that Mother Nature may mend it and make the leg or arm as good as ever. But with the little people of the Green Forest and the Green Meadows, nothing of this sort is possible, and very, very often a broken limb means an early death. You see, such a break will not mend properly, and the little sufferer becomes a cripple, and cripples cannot long escape their enemies.

So, though he didn't know it at the time, it was a very lucky thing for Bobby Coon that Farmer Brown's boy discovered that broken leg and wrapped him up in his coat and took him home. Bobby didn't think it was lucky. Oh, my, no! Bobby thought it was just the other way about. You see, he didn't know Farmer Brown's boy, except by sight. He didn't know of his gentleness and tender heart. All he knew of men and boys was that most of them seemed to delight in hunting him, in frightening him and trying to kill him. So all through that strange journey in the arms of Farmer Brown's boy, up to Farmer Brown's barn, Bobby was sure, absolutely sure, that he was being taken somewhere to be killed. He didn't have a doubt, not the least doubt, of it.

When they reached the barn, Farmer Brown's boy put Bobby down very gently, but fastened him in the coat so that he couldn't get out. Then he went to the house and presently returned with some neat strips of clean white cloth. Then he took out his knife and made very smooth two thin, flat sticks. When these suited him, he tied Bobby's hind legs together so that he couldn't kick with them.

Then he placed Bobby on his side on a board and with a broad strip of cloth bound him to it in such a way that Bobby couldn't move. All the time he talked to Bobby in the gentlest of voices and did his best not to hurt him.

But Bobby couldn't understand, and to be wholly helpless, not to be able to kick or scratch or bite, was the most dreadful feeling he ever had known. He was sure that something worse was about to happen. You see, he didn't know anything about doctors, and so of course he couldn't know that Farmer Brown's boy was playing doctor. Very, very gently Farmer Brown's boy felt of the broken leg. He brought the broken parts together, and when he was sure that they just fitted, he bound them in place on one of the thin, smooth, flat sticks with one of the strips of clean white cloth. Then he put the other smooth flat stick above the break and wound the whole about with strips of cloth so tightly that there was no chance for those two sticks to slip. That was so that the two parts of the broken bone in the leg would be held just where they belonged until they could grow together. When it was done to suit him, he covered the outside with something very, very bitter and bad-tasting. This was to keep Bobby from trying to tear off the cloth with his teeth. You see, he knew that if that leg was to become as good as ever it was, it must stay just as he had bound it until Old Mother Nature could heal it.

So Farmer Brown's boy played doctor, and a very gentle and kindly doctor he was, for his heart was full of pity for poor Bobby Coon.

CHAPTER IX

Bobby Is Made Much Of

There's nothing like a stomach full
To make the world seem brighter;
To banish worry, drive out fear,
And make the heart feel lighter.

While Farmer Brown's boy was playing doctor and doing his best to fix Bobby Coon's broken leg so that it would heal and be as good as ever, poor Bobby was wholly in despair, and nothing is more dreadful than to be wholly in despair. There he was, perfectly helpless, for Farmer Brown's boy had bound him so that he couldn't move. You see, Bobby couldn't understand what it all meant. If he could have understood Farmer Brown's boy, it would have been very different. But he couldn't, and so his mind was all the time full of dreadful fear.

When Farmer Brown's boy had bound that broken leg so that it would be held firmly in place to heal, he made a comfortable bed in a deep box out of which Bobby couldn't possibly climb with that broken leg. In this he put Bobby very gently, after taking off the bands with which he had been bound to the board while the broken leg was being fixed. Then he went to the house and presently returned with more good things to eat than Bobby had seen since cold weather began. These he put in the box with Bobby, and then left him alone.

Now at first Bobby made up his mind that he wouldn't taste so much as a crumb. He would starve rather than live a prisoner, which was what he felt himself to be. But his stomach was empty, the smell of those good things tickled his nose, and in spite of himself he began to nibble. The first thing he knew he had filled his stomach, the first good meal he had had for many weeks, because, you know, he had been asleep most of the winter.

Right away Bobby felt sleepy. A full stomach, you know, almost always makes one feel sleepy. Then, too, Bobby was quite tired out with the fright and strange experience he had been through. So he curled up, and in no time at all he had forgotten all his troubles. And for days and days

Bobby slept most of the time. You see, he was finishing out that long winter sleep he was used to. And this, it happens, was the very best thing in the world for Bobby. Being asleep, he wasn't tempted to try to pull off that bandage around the broken leg, and so the leg had just the chance it needed to mend.

Every day Farmer Brown's boy visited Bobby, just as a good doctor should visit a patient, and looked carefully at the bandaged leg to make sure that it was as it should be. And whenever Farmer Brown's boy visited Bobby, he took some goody in his pocket to tempt Bobby's appetite, just as if it needed tempting! Bobby would wake up long enough to eat what had been brought and then would go to sleep again, quite as if he were all alone.

As the weather grew warmer, Bobby grew more wakeful. Of course, he had plenty of time in which to remember and to think. He remembered how dreadfully frightened he had been when Farmer Brown's boy had caught him and brought him to the barn, all because he had not really known Farmer Brown's boy. Now everything was different, so very, very different. It was a fact, an actual fact, that

Bobby had learned to know the step of Farmer Brown's boy, and when he heard it coming his way, he was as tickled as once he would have been frightened. You see, Farmer Brown's boy was very, very good to him and made so much of him that I am afraid he was quite spoiling Bobby. Kindness had driven out fear from Bobby's mind, and in its place had come trust. It will do it every time, if given a chance.

CHAPTER X

Bobby Longs for the Green Forest

Now though Bobby Coon was made a great deal of by Farmer Brown's boy, and was petted and stuffed with good things to eat until it was a wonder that he wasn't made sick, he was really a prisoner. Excepting when Farmer Brown's boy played with him in the house, he was fastened by a long chain. You see, when at last the bandage was taken off, and the leg was found to have healed, Bobby was kept a prisoner that he might get the full use of that leg once more before having to shift for himself. Day by day the strength came back to that leg until it was as good as ever it had been, and still Bobby was kept a prisoner. The truth is, Farmer Brown's boy had grown so fond of Bobby that he couldn't bear to think of parting with him.

At first, Bobby hadn't minded in the least. It was fine to have all the good things to eat he wanted without the trouble of hunting for them, things he never had had before and never could have in the Green Forest. It was fine to have a warm, comfortable bed and not a thing in the world to worry about. So for a time Bobby was quite content to be a prisoner. He didn't mind that chain at all, excepting when he wanted to poke his inquisitive little nose into something he couldn't reach.

But as sweet Mistress Spring awakened those who had slept the long winter away—the trees and flowers and insects, and Old Mr. Toad and Johnny Chuck and Striped Chipmunk and all the rest—and as one after another the birds arrived from the sunny Southland, and Bobby heard them singing and twittering, and watched them flying about, a great longing for the Green Forest crept into his heart.

At first he didn't really know what it was that he wanted. It simply made him uneasy. He couldn't keep still. He walked back and forth, back and forth, at the length of his chain. He began to lose his appetite. Then one day Farmer Brown's boy brought him a fish for his dinner, and all in a flash Bobby knew what it was he wanted. He wanted to go back to the Green Forest. He wanted to fish for himself in the Laughing Brook. He wanted to climb trees. He wanted to visit his old neighbors and see what they were doing. He wanted to hunt for bugs under old logs and around old stumps. He wanted to hunt for nests being built, so that later he might steal the eggs from them. Yes, he did just this, I am sorry to say. Bobby is very fond of eggs, and he considers that he has a perfect right to them if he is smart enough to find them. He wanted to be *free*—free to do what he pleased when he pleased and how he pleased. He wanted to go back home to the Green Forest.

"Farmer Brown's boy has been very good to me, and I believe he would let me go if only I could tell him what I want," thought Bobby, "but I can't make him understand what I say any more than I can understand what he says. What a great pity it is that we don't all speak the same language. Then we would all understand each other, and I don't believe we little folks of the Green Forest and the Green Meadows would be hunted so much by these men creatures. There's nothing like common speech to make folks understand one another. I know Farmer Brown's boy would let me go if he only knew; I *know* he would."

Bobby sat down where he could look over towards the Green Forest and sighed and sighed, and all the longing of his heart crept into his eyes.

CHAPTER XI

The Happiest Coon Ever

As jolly Mr. Sun smiles down
  And makes the land all bright and fair
So happiness within the heart
  Spreads joy and gladness everywhere.

Now though Bobby Coon couldn't speak the language of Farmer Brown's boy and so tell him how he longed to be free and go back to the Green Forest, he could and he did tell him in another way just what was in his heart. He told him with his eyes, though he didn't know it. You know eyes are sometimes called the windows of the soul. This means simply that as you look out through your eyes and see all that is going on about you, so others may sometimes look right in your eyes and see what is going on within your mind. Eyes are very wonderful things, and a great deal may be learned from them. Eyes will tell the truth when a tongue is busy telling a wrong

Unc' Billy Possum and old Mrs. Possum didn't want to move.

See page 50

story. I guess you know how hard it is when you have done wrong to look mother straight in the face and try to make her believe that you haven't done wrong. That is because your eyes are truthful.

Looking straight into the eyes of fierce wild animals often will fill them with fear. Trainers of lions and other dangerous animals know this and do it a great deal. Fear will show in the eyes when it shows nowhere else. It is the same with happiness and contentment. So it is with sorrow and worry. Just as a thermometer shows just how warm it is or how cold it is, so the eyes show our feelings. So when Bobby Coon sat down and gazed towards the Green Forest and wished that he could tell Farmer Brown's boy how he wanted to go back there, a look of longing grew and grew in Bobby's eyes, and Farmer Brown's boy saw it. What is more, he understood it. His own eyes grew soft.

"You poor little rascal," said he, "I believe you think you are a prisoner and that you want to go back home. Well, I guess there is no reason why you shouldn't now. I'm very fond of you, Bobby. Yes, I am. I'm so fond of you that I hate to have you go, and I guess that I've kept you longer than was necessary. That leg of yours looks to me to be as good as ever, so I really haven't an excuse for keeping you any longer. I think we'll take a walk this afternoon."

If Bobby could have understood what Farmer Brown's boy was saying, it would have made him feel a great deal better. But he didn't understand, and so he continued to stare towards the Green Forest and grow more and more homesick. After dinner, Farmer Brown's boy came out and took off the collar and chain, and picked Bobby up in his arms. This time Bobby didn't have his eyes covered as he did when he had been brought from the Green Forest. Fear no longer made him want to bite and scratch. Through the Old Orchard straight to the Green Forest they went, and Bobby began to grow excited. What was going to happen? What did it mean?

Through the Green Forest straight to the place where Bobby's great hollow tree used to stand went Farmer Brown's boy.

When they got there he smoothed Bobby's coat and

patted him gently. Then he put him down on the ground.

"Here we are, Bobby," said he. "Now run along and find a new house and be happy. I hope you won't forget me, because I am going to come over often to see you. Just keep out of mischief, and above all keep out of the way of hunters next fall. They shall not hunt here if I can help it, but you know I cannot watch all the time. Good-by, Bobby, and take care of yourself."

Bobby didn't say good-by, because he didn't know how. But a great joy came into his eyes, and Farmer Brown's boy saw it and understood. Straight off among the trees Bobby walked. Once he looked back. Farmer Brown's boy was watching him and waved a hand.

"He was good to me. He certainly was good to me," thought Bobby. "I—I believe I really am very fond of him."

Then he went on to look for a new house. All the joy of the springtime was in his heart. He was free! He was home once more in the Green Forest! He no longer feared Farmer Brown's boy!

"I'm the happiest Coon in all the world!" cried Bobby.

CHAPTER XII

Bobby Tries the Wrong House

"Home again! Home again! Happy am I!
Had I but wings I most surely would fly!"

So sang Bobby Coon as he wandered about in the Green Forest after leaving Farmer Brown's boy. At least, he meant it for singing. Of course, it wasn't real singing, for Bobby Coon can no more sing than he can fly. But it did very well to express his happiness, and that was all it was intended to do. Bobby was happy. He was very happy indeed. Indeed he couldn't remember ever having been quite so happy. You see, he never before had understood fully what freedom means. No one can fully understand what a wonderful and blessed thing freedom is until they have lost it and then got it again.

Bobby took long breaths and sniffed and sniffed and sniffed and sniffed the sweet smells of early spring. The Green Forest was full of them, and never had they seemed

46

so good to Bobby. He climbed a tree for nothing under the sun but to know what it felt like to climb once more. Then he climbed down to earth again and went poking around among the leaves just for the fun of poking around. He rolled over and over from sheer joy. Finally he brushed himself off, climbed up on an old stump, and sat down to think things over.

"Of course," said he to himself, "the first thing for me to do is to find a new house. I don't have to have it right away, because there are plenty of places in which I can curl up for a nap, but it is more convenient and much more respectable to have a house. People who sleep anywhere and have no homes are never thought much of by their friends and neighbors. Without a home I can have no self-respect. There's a certain old hollow tree I always did like the looks of. Unc' Billy Possum used to live there, but maybe he has moved. Anyway, he may be out, and if so he will be smarter than I think he is to get me out once I'm inside. I believe I'll look up that tree right away."

Bobby scrambled down from the stump and started down the Lone Little Path. After a while he turned off the Lone Little Path into a hollow and presently came to the tree he had in mind. It was straight, tall, and big. High up was a doorway plenty big enough for Bobby Coon. He sat down and looked up. The longer he looked, the better that tree seemed to him. It would suit for a house first-rate. There were marks on the tree made by claws—the claws of Unc' Billy Possum. Some of them looked quite fresh.

"Looks as if Unc' Billy is still living here," thought Bobby. "Well, I can't help it if he is. If that tree looks as good inside as it does outside, I am afraid Unc' Billy and I will have a falling out. It's everyone for himself in the Green Forest, and I don't think Unc' Billy will care to fight me. I'm bigger and considerably stronger than he, so if he's there, I guess I'll just invite him to move out."

Now, of course, this wasn't at all right of Bobby Coon, but it is the way things are done in the Green Forest, and the people who live there are used to it. The strong take what they want if they can get it, and Bobby knew that Unc' Billy Possum would treat Happy Jack Squirrel the same way, if he happened to want Happy Jack's house.

Out of the old log backed Bobby Coon, followed by Prickly Porky
the Porcupine. *See page 55*

So he climbed up the tree, quite sure that this was the house he would take for his new home. He was half-way up when a sharp voice spoke.

"Haven't yo' made a mistake, Brer Coon?" said the voice. "This isn't your house."

Bobby stopped and looked up. Unc' Billy Possum was grinning down at him from his doorway. Bobby grinned back. "It occurred to me that you might like to move, and as I'm looking for a house, I think this one will suit me very well," said he, and grinned again, for he knew that Unc' Billy would understand just what he meant.

Before Unc' Billy could say a word, another sharp face appeared beside his own, and a voice still sharper than his said: "What's that no 'count Coon doing in our tree? What's this talk Ah hear about moving? Isn't nobody gwine to move that Ah knows of."

Bobby had forgotten all about old Mrs. Possum, and now as he saw that it was two against one he suddenly changed his mind.

"Excuse me," said he, "I guess I've got the wrong house."

CHAPTER XIII

Bobby Makes Another Mistake

When Bobby Coon left Unc' Billy Possum's hollow tree, he went fishing. You know he is very fond of fishing. All night long he fished and played along the Laughing Brook, and when at last jolly, round, red Mr. Sun began his daily climb up in the blue, blue sky, Bobby was wet, tired, and sleepy. But he was happy. It did seem so good to be wandering about at his own sweet will in the beautiful Green Forest once more. It struck him now as rather a joke that he hadn't any house to go to. It was a long, long time since he had been without a home.

"I've got to sleep somewhere," said Bobby, rubbing his eyes and yawning, "and the sooner I find a place, the better. I'm so sleepy now I can hardly keep my eyes open. Hello, there's a great big log over there! If it is hollow, it will be just the place for me."

He marched straight over to the old log. It was big,

51

very big, and to Bobby's great joy it was hollow, with an opening at one end. He was just going to crawl in, when Peter Rabbit popped out from behind a tree.

"Hello, Bobby Coon!" cried Peter joyously. "Where have you been? I was over where you used to live and found your house gone, and I was afraid something dreadful had happened to you. What did happen, and where have you been?"

Now, tired and sleepy as he was, Bobby had to stop and talk for a few minutes. You see, Peter was the first of his friends Bobby had met to whom he could tell all the wonderful things that had happened to him, and he was fairly aching to tell someone. So he sat down and told Peter how his hollow tree had been cut down, and how his leg had been broken, and how Farmer Brown's boy had taken him home and fixed that leg so that Old Mother Nature could make it as well and sound as ever, and how Farmer Brown's boy had brought him back to the Green Forest and set him free, and how he had been fishing all night and now was looking for a place to get a wink or two of sleep.

"Now, if you'll excuse me, Peter, I'm going to turn in

for a nap," Bobby ended, and started to crawl in the end of the hollow log.

"Oh!" cried Peter. "Oh, you mustn't go in there, Bobby!"

But Bobby didn't hear him, or if he did he didn't heed. He kept right on and disappeared. A funny look crept over Peter's face, and presently he began to chuckle. "I think I'll wait a while and see what happens," said he.

Inside that big hollow log, Bobby found it very dry and warm and comfortable. There was a bed of dry leaves there, and it looked very inviting. Now ordinarily Bobby would have examined the inside of that log very thoroughly before going to sleep, but he was so tired and sleepy that he didn't half look around. He didn't go to the farther end at all. He just dropped right down midway, curled up, and in no time at all was fast asleep. It was a mistake, a very great mistake, as Bobby was shortly to find out. Meanwhile, outside sat Peter Rabbit, although it was already past time for him to be home in the dear Old Briar-patch.

CHAPTER XIV

Bobby Finds Out His Mistake

If friend of yours a mistake makes
Nor yet has found it out,
I pray that when at last he does
You will not be about.

It is bad enough to find out for yourself that you have made a mistake, but to have other people know it makes you feel a great deal worse. So the kindest thing that any-one can do when they know a friend has made a mistake and it is too late to warn them, is to appear not to know of it at all. So it wasn't nice at all of Peter Rabbit to hang around watching that old hollow log into which Bobby Coon had crawled for a nap.

Presently Peter's long ears caught sounds from inside that hollow log. First there was a rattling and rustling. Then came a series of grunts and squeaks. These were followed by growls and snarls. The latter were from Bobby

54

Coon. He was insisting that he was going to stay right where he was and wouldn't move an inch for anyone. Peter clapped one hand over his mouth to keep from laughing aloud when he heard that, and he fastened his eyes, very big and round with expectation, on the opening in the end of the hollow log. You see, Peter knew all about that log and who lived there. That is what he had tried to tell Bobby Coon. He could hear Bobby declaring:

"I won't move a step, not a single step. You can stay right where you are until I finish my nap. If you come any nearer, I'll—"

Peter didn't hear the rest, if indeed Bobby finished what he had started to say. You see, Bobby was interrupted by a great rattling and rustling and a grunt that sounded both angry and very business-like. Once more Bobby growled and snarled and declared he wouldn't move a step, but Peter noticed that Bobby's voice seemed to come from nearer the open end of the log than before. Again there was a grunt and a rattling and rustling.

Then out of the end of the old log backed Bobby Coon, still growling and snarling and declaring he wouldn't move a step. It was too funny for Peter to hold in any longer. He had to laugh. He couldn't help it. Then the black nose and little dull eyes of Prickly Porky the Porcupine appeared. In each of those little dull eyes there was just a wee spark of anger which made them less dull than usual. It was plain that Prickly Porky was provoked.

As soon as he was outside, he made the thousand little spears which he carries hidden in his coat stand on end, and made a quick little rush towards Bobby Coon. Bobby turned tail and ran. The sight of those sharp-pointed little spears was too much for him. He was afraid of them. Everybody is afraid of them, even big Buster Bear. It was these little spears brushing against the inside of the old log that had made the rattling and rustling Peter had heard.

"The impudence of that Coon to walk into my house and go to sleep without so much as asking if he might, and then telling me that I can't come out until he says so! The impudence of him!" grunted Prickly Porky, rattling his thousand little spears.

As for Bobby Coon, he realized now the great mistake he had made in not first finding out whether anyone was at home in that old log before trying to take a nap there. It mortified him to think he had been so careless as to make such a mistake, and it mortified him still more to know that Peter Rabbit had seen all that had happened.

CHAPTER XV

Once More Bobby Tries to Sleep

Did you ever have the Sandman
Fill your eyes all full of sand
And then have to keep them open
When there was no bed at hand?

If you have had that happen, then you know exactly how Bobby Coon felt when he was obliged to crawl out of Prickly Porky's bed and go hunt for another. He was so very, very sleepy that he felt almost as if he could go to sleep standing right on his feet. This was because he had been up all night and awake most of the day before. Now he wished that instead of spending the night in fishing and playing about the Laughing Brook, he had hunted for a house.

To be sleepy and not able to sleep makes Bobby cross, just as it does most folks. So, as he hurried away from the neighborhood of Prickly Porky and his thousand little

58

spears, he was in a bad temper. Of course, he knew it was his own fault that he was in such a fix, and this didn't make him feel a bit better. In fact, it made him feel worse. It usually is that way.

So he grumbled to himself as he went along. He didn't know where he was going. He was too cross and sleepy and upset to do any thinking. So he went along, aimlessly looking for a place where he might sleep undisturbed. At last he came to a tall stump, a great big old stump that had stood in the Green Forest for years and years. Bobby climbed to the top of it. It was hollow, just as he had hoped. Indeed, it was just a shell. Looking down, Bobby saw with a great deal of satisfaction that the bottom was covered with a great mass of rotted wood. It would make a very comfortable bed. Moreover, it was plain that no one else was using it.

Bobby sighed with satisfaction. It was just the place for a good long nap. He could sleep there all day in perfect comfort. It wouldn't do for a home, because the top was open to the sky, and on a rainy day the inside of that stump would soon be a very wet place indeed. But for a nice long nap on a pleasant day, it would be hard to beat. Bobby sighed again, looked all about to make sure that no one was watching him, and then climbed down inside.

"I guess," muttered Bobby, as he curled up on the bed of rotted wood, which is sometimes called punk, "that at last I shall be allowed to sleep in peace. I never was more sleepy in all my life." He yawned two or three times, changed his position for greater comfort, closed his eyes, and in a twinkling was asleep.

Now, though he thought no one saw him go into that old stump, someone did. That someone was Peter Rabbit. Peter had followed Bobby just out of curiosity. He had hidden behind trees so as to keep out of Bobby's sight. So he had seen Bobby climb the stump and disappear inside.

"I guess," said Peter, "that this time he will sleep in peace. No one is likely to find him there unless it should be that Sammy Jay or Blacky the Crow happens to fly over and so discover him. They wouldn't give him a bit of peace if they should. Hello! There's Blacky's voice now, and he seems to be coming this way. I think I will hang around a while longer."

CHAPTER XVI

Blacky the Crow Discovers Bobby

Blacky the Crow is sharp of eye;
He dearly loves to peek and pry.
I must confess, alas! alack!
Blacky the Crow's an imp in black.

It is true, I am sorry to say, that Blacky the Crow never is happier than when he is teasing someone and making him uncomfortable. He is an imp of mischief, is Blacky. Whatever business he has on hand he goes about it with one eye open for a chance to have fun at the expense of someone else. And there is little that those sharp eyes of his miss. He sees all that there is to see. Yes, sir, you may trust Blacky for that!

It was just the hard luck of Bobby Coon that no sooner was he asleep in that hollow stump in the Green Forest than along came Blacky the Crow, flying above the tree-tops on his way to his nest, but as usual watching sharply

61

for what might be going on below. It just happened that he flew right over that stump, so that he could look right down inside. He saw Bobby Coon curled up there asleep. Yes, indeed, you may be sure he saw Bobby.

Blacky checked himself in his flight and hovered for an instant right above that stump. Mischief fairly danced in his sharp eyes. Then he turned and silently flew down and alighted on the edge of the old stump. For a few minutes he sat there, looking down at Bobby Coon. All the time he was chuckling to himself. Then he flew to the top of a tree and began to call with all his might.

"Caw caw, caw, ca-a-w, caw, caw!" he called. "Caw, ca-a-w, caw!"

Almost right away he was answered, and presently from all directions came hurrying his friends and relatives, each one cawing at the top of his voice and asking Blacky what he had found. Blacky didn't tell them until the last one came hurrying up. Then he told them to go look in the old hollow stump. One after another they flew over it, looking down, and one after another they shouted with glee. Then as many as could find a place on the edge of the

The old stump gave way, and out rolled Bobby Coon. *See page 68*

old stump did so, while the others sat about in the trees or flew back and forth overhead, and all of them began to caw as hard as ever they could. Such a racket as they made!

Of course, Bobby Coon couldn't sleep. Certainly not. No one could have slept through that racket. He opened his eyes and looked up. He saw a ring of black heads looking down at him and mischief fairly dancing in the sharp eyes watching him. The instant it was known that he was awake, the noise redoubled.

"Ca-a-w, ca-a-w, ca-a-w, caw, caw, ca-a-w, caw, caw, caw!"

Bobby drew back his lips and snarled, and at that his tormentors fairly shrieked with glee. Then Blacky dropped a little stick down on Bobby. Another crow did the same thing. Bobby scrambled to his feet and started to climb up. His tormentors took to the air and screamed louder than ever. Bobby stopped. What was the use of going up where they could get at him? They would pull his fur and make him most uncomfortable, and he knew he couldn't catch one of them to save him. He backed down and sat glaring up at them and telling them what dreadful things he would do to them if ever he should catch one of them. This delighted Blacky and his friends more than ever. They certainly were having great fun.

Finally Bobby did the wisest thing possible. He once more curled up and took no notice at all of the black imps. Of course, he couldn't go to sleep with such a racket going on, but he pretended to sleep. Now you know there is no fun in trying to tease one who won't show he is teased. After a while Blacky and his friends got tired of screaming. They had had their fun, and one by one they flew about their business until at last the Green Forest was as still as still could be. Bobby sighed thankfully and once more fell asleep.

CHAPTER XVII

The Surprise of Two Cousins

Peter Rabbit should have been back home in the dear Old Briar-patch long ago. He knew that Mrs. Peter was worrying. She always worries when Peter overstays. But Peter was not giving much thought to Mrs. Peter. In fact, I am afraid he was not giving any thought to her. You see, he was too full of curiosity about Bobby Coon and what might happen to him. He had been sorry for Bobby in a way, yet it had seemed like a great joke that anyone as sleepy as Bobby was shouldn't be able to sleep. So I am afraid Peter rather enjoyed the excitement.

When finally Blacky and his friends grew tired and went about their business, Peter began to think of getting back to the dear Old Briar-patch.

"I guess Bobby will sleep in peace now," thought Peter. "I can't think of anything more that possibly can happen to disturb him. Poor Bobby. He has had a hard time getting that nap."

66

Still Peter hung around. He didn't know just why, but he had a feeling that he might miss something if he left, and you know Peter never could forgive himself if he missed anything worth seeing. So he hung around for some time after Blacky and his friends had gone about their business. At last he had just about made up his mind that he had better be starting for home when he was startled by the snapping of a little twig. Peeping out from behind a big tree, Peter stared towards the place from which that sound had come. In a moment he saw a big black form.

"Buster Bear!" gasped Peter. "It's the first time I have seen him this spring. My, how thin he is!"

Peter looked about to make sure that the way was clear for a hasty run if it should be necessary, and then held his breath as Buster drew near. Buster kept stopping to look and listen and sniff the air, and suddenly Peter understood.

"He heard those noisy Crows, and he has come to see what it was all about," thought Peter, which was just exactly the case.

Buster knew that it was just about this place that Blacky and his friends had been making such a racket, and his greedy little eyes searched everywhere for some sign of what had been going on. But there was nothing to be seen but a black feather at the foot of a tall old stump. By this Buster knew for sure that he had found the place where Blacky and his friends had been, but there was nothing to tell him why they had been there. Buster sat up and blinked thoughtfully. Then as he looked at the old stump, his eyes brightened.

"I don't know what all that fuss was about," he muttered, "and I guess I never will know, but I'm glad I came just the same. That old stump looks to me to be rotten and hollow. I have found ant nests in many an old stump like that, and beetles and grubs. I'll just see what this one contains."

Buster walked over to the old stump, hooked his great claws into a crack, and pulled with all his might. Peter Rabbit, watching, held his breath with excitement. There was a sharp cracking sound, and then the whole side of that old stump gave way so suddenly that Buster Bear fell over backwards. As he did so, Bobby Coon rolled out, half awake and frightened almost out of his wits. It was hard to say which was the most surprised of those two cousins, Buster Bear or Bobby Coon.

CHAPTER XVIII

Buster Bear's Short Temper

It's such a very foolish thing,
     So silly and so heedless,
To lose your temper when you know
     It is so wholly needless.

When Buster Bear scrambled to his feet and saw his cousin, Bobby Coon, scrambling to his feet, Buster straightway lost his temper. It was a foolish thing to do, a very foolish thing to do. There really wasn't the least excuse in the world for it. And yet Buster mustn't be blamed too much. You see, he wasn't really himself. Ordinarily Buster is one of the best-natured people in all the Green Forest. He doesn't begin to be as short-tempered as ever so many others are. In fact, he isn't short-tempered at all.

But just now Buster was hungry. He was so hungry that he couldn't think of anything but his stomach and how empty it was. You see, so early in the spring there was very

70

little for him to eat, and he had to hunt and hunt to find that little. When he had started to tear open that tall old stump, he had hoped that inside he would find either a nest of ants, or some of the worms and insects that like to bury themselves in rotting wood. So when Bobby Coon came rolling out, Buster was so disappointed that he quite lost his temper before he had time to think. He flew into a rage. You see, he just took it for granted that Bobby Coon had been in that hollow stump for the very same purpose that he had torn it open. Now it never does to take things for granted. You know and I know that Bobby Coon had crawled into that stump only to sleep.

Buster didn't know this, and Buster didn't stop to find it out. He growled a terribly deep, ugly-sounding growl that made all of Peter Rabbit's hair stand on end. You know, Peter was close by, hiding behind a big tree to see all that might happen. Then Buster Bear started for his cousin, Bobby Coon, and his little eyes seemed to fairly snap fire.

"I'll teach you to steal an honest bear's dinner!" he growled in his deep, grumbly, rumbly voice.

Now this wasn't fair to Bobby, for Bobby had stolen no

dinner. Even if he had been hunting for food in that hollow stump, he would have done no injustice to Buster Bear. But Buster didn't stop to think of this.

"You'll pay for it by furnishing me a dinner yourself!" growled Buster.

"But I'm your cousin!" cried Bobby, as he started to run.

"That doesn't make a bit of difference," snapped Buster. "I'm hungry enough to eat my own brother if I had one."

All the time Buster was scrambling after Bobby Coon, and Bobby was running for his life. Now big as he is, Buster can move very fast when he is in a hurry, especially when he is thin and lean. Bobby Coon squealed with fright and scrambled up a big tree faster than he ever had scrambled up a tree before in all his life. Buster growled a deep, grumbly, rumbly growl and started up after him.

"Oh! Oh!" cried Bobby Coon, and you may be sure he was very much awake by this time. There was no thought of sleep in Bobby's head as he scrambled nearly to the top of that big tree. Peter Rabbit stared in horror. Surely Buster Bear would catch Bobby now!

CHAPTER XIX

Bobby Coon Gets a Terrible Shaking

"Leave me alone! I've never done you any harm, so leave me alone!" whimpered Bobby Coon, as he climbed the tall tree with Buster Bear scrambling up after him and growling all the way. For a minute or two Bobby wished he had stayed on the ground. You see, he had forgotten that Buster Bear could climb quite as well as he could. Now he was in the tree, and Buster was below him, and it looked very much as if Bobby had trapped himself.

Suddenly he remembered that Buster couldn't go out on little branches as he could, because Buster was too big and heavy. Bobby looked about him, and fear made his eyes quick to see. One branch reached over almost to the top of a slender young tree growing near. If he could get over into that tree, perhaps he could get back to the ground and run for his life. Anyway, it was worth trying. Out along the branch went Bobby as far as he could, and then,

73

with his heart in his mouth, he jumped for the slender young tree. It was a good jump, and he caught hold of a branch of the young tree. Then he turned to see what Buster Bear was about.

Now there is nothing slow about Buster Bear's wits. The moment he saw Bobby run out on that branch, he knew just what was in Bobby's mind.

"Huh!" grunted Buster to himself. "If he thinks he can catch me napping with such an old trick as that, he will have to think again."

He waited only long enough to make sure that Bobby would jump for the other tree, and then Buster went down faster than he had come up. You see, he just dropped for the last half of the distance. So by the time Bobby Coon was half-way down the slender tree, Buster Bear was at the foot of it, waiting for him. Poor Bobby! At first he thought he was no better off than before. There was no other tree he could reach from this one. Now all Buster would have to do would be to climb up and get him. Bobby was about ready to give up in despair.

But Buster didn't climb up. He didn't even try. He just

stood there at the foot of the tree and growled. Every growl made a shiver of fright run all over Bobby. Why didn't Buster hurry up and get him? All in a flash it came to Bobby why Buster didn't. He didn't because he couldn't! That was the reason. He couldn't climb that tree because it was too *small* for him to climb. He is such a big fellow that he has to have a good-sized tree to get his arms around. Once more Bobby began to hope.

But Buster Bear isn't one to give up easily. No, sir, Buster doesn't give up until he has tried all the things he can think of. Now he stood up and took hold of that tree almost as if he were going to try to climb it. At first Bobby thought he was, but in a minute he found out his mistake. Buster began to shake that tree. My, my, my, how he did shake it! He was trying to shake Bobby Coon down.

The very first shake caught Bobby by surprise, and he very nearly lost his hold. Then he saw what Buster was up to, and he held on for dear life. He held on with arms and legs and teeth. Back and forth swung that tree and Bobby with it. It was worse, very much worse, than the hardest wind Bobby ever had been out in. But he grimly held on

with claws and teeth, and over and over he said to himself:
"I won't let go. I won't let go. I won't let go." And
he didn't.

CHAPTER XX

Peter Rabbit Saves Bobby Coon

There are heroes who are heroes
First in thought and then in fact.
Others are made into heroes;
Quite by accident, in fact.

Real heroes are those who do brave deeds, knowing
all the time just what they are about, what risks they are
taking, what will happen if they fail, and yet do the brave
deeds just the same. The other kind of heroes are not real,
true heroes at all, but are treated as if they were and are
made just as much of as if they were. They are the ones who
do what seem to be brave deeds, but which in truth haven't
been planned at all and have been done unintentionally.
People who, in trying to save their own lives, happen to save
the lives of others, always are called heroes and are looked
up to and made much of when in truth they are not heroes
at all.

77

Bobby jumped for the slender young tree. *See page 73*

Peter Rabbit is this kind of a hero. He saved Bobby Coon's life. At least, Bobby Coon is kind enough to say he did. Anyway, he made it possible for Bobby to escape from angry Buster Bear. So Peter is called a hero and has been made much of. Everybody says that he was very, very brave. But right down in his own heart, Peter knows that he doesn't deserve any of the nice things said about him. True, he did save Bobby Coon, but he didn't do it purposely. No, sir. Perhaps he might have, if he had thought of it, but he didn't think of it. What he did wasn't the result of thinking and planning at all, but of not thinking; of carelessness and heedlessness, if you please. But it made a hero of Peter in the eyes of his friends and neighbors just the same. You see, it was this way:

When Buster Bear began to shake that slender young tree, trying to shake Bobby Coon out of it, Peter forgot everything but his desire to see what would happen. From where he crouched, behind that big tree, he couldn't clearly see Bobby Coon in the top of the slender young tree. So, quite forgetting that he might be in danger himself, Peter hopped out from behind that big tree to try to find a place where he could see better. In his curiosity and excitement, he heedlessly forgot to watch his steps and trod on a dry stick. It broke with a little snap.

Now, no one in all the Green Forest has keener ears than Buster Bear. In spite of the fact that his attention was all on Bobby Coon, he heard that little snap and whirled like a flash to see what had made it. There sat round-eyed Peter Rabbit, staring with all his might. Without pausing an instant, Buster sprang for Peter. He would make very good eating, as Buster well knew, and a Rabbit on the ground was better than a Coon he couldn't shake out of a tree.

Peter dodged just in time and with a squeal of fear away he went, lipperty-lipperty-lip, twisting, dodging, running with all his might, and after him crashed Buster Bear. How Peter did wish that he hadn't been so curious, but had gone home to the dear Old Briar-patch when he should have! He was too frightened to know when Buster Bear gave up the chase, but kept right on running. As a matter of fact, Buster didn't chase him far. He knew that Peter was too nimble for him to catch in a tail-end race. So presently he gave it up and hurried back. Bobby Coon was nowhere in sight. He had taken the chance to climb down from that tree and run away. By leading Buster off for just those few minutes, Peter had saved Bobby Coon, and though he hadn't done it purposely, he got the credit just the same. He became a hero. This is a funny old world, isn't it?

CHAPTER XXI

Bobby Finds a Home at Last

The very instant Buster Bear started after Peter Rabbit, down from that tree scrambled Bobby Coon. Never in all his life had he scrambled down a tree faster. He knew that Buster would not follow Peter far, and so he, Bobby, had no time to lose. He would get just as far from that place as he could before Buster should return.

So while Peter Rabbit was running, lipperty-lipperty-lip, in one direction as fast as ever he could, Bobby Coon was running in the opposite direction, and his black feet were moving astonishingly fast. He didn't know where he was going, but he was on his way somewhere, anywhere, to get out of the neighborhood of Buster Bear. So Bobby took little heed of where he was going, but ran until he was too tired to run any more. His heart was beating thumpity-thump-thump, thumpity-thump-thump, and he was breathing so hard that every breath was a gasp and hurt.

He just had to stop. He couldn't run another step.

After a while Bobby's heart stopped going thumpity-thumpity-thump, and he once more breathed easily. He knew that he had escaped. He was safe. He sighed, and that sigh was a happy little sigh. Then he grinned. He was thinking of how hard he had tried to get a chance to sleep that day, and how every time he thought he had found a bed, he had been turned out of it almost as soon as he had closed his eyes. Bobby has a sense of fun, and now he saw the funny side of all his experiences.

"There is one thing sure, and that is being without a home is a more serious matter than I thought it was," said he. "I thought it would be easy enough to find a place to sleep when I wanted to, but I've begun to think that it is about the hardest thing I've ever tried to do. Here I am in a strange part of the Green Forest and homeless. There's no use in going back where I used to live, so I may as well look around here and see what I can find. Perhaps there is an empty house somewhere near. Most anything will do for a while."

So Bobby began to look about for an empty house. Now,

of course, he had in mind a hollow tree or log. He always had lived in a hollow tree, and so he preferred one now. But he soon found that hollow trees were few and far between in that part of the Green Forest, and those he did find didn't have hollows big enough for him. The same thing was true of hollow logs. He was getting discouraged when he came to a ledge of rock which was the foundation of a little hill deep in the Green Forest.

In this ledge of rock Bobby discovered a crack big enough for him to squeeze into. Just out of curiosity he did squeeze into it, and then he discovered that after a little it grew wider and formed the snuggest little cave he ever had seen. It was very dry and comfortable in there. All in a flash it came to Bobby that the only thing needed to make this the snuggest kind of a house was a bed of dry leaves, and these were easy to get. Bobby's eyes danced.

"I've found my new home," he declared out loud. "It can't be cut down as my old home was; Buster Bear can't tear it open with his great claws; no one bigger than I can get into it. It's the safest and best house in all the Green Forest, and I'm going to stay right here."

Right then and there Bobby Coon curled up for that sleep he so much needed.

CHAPTER XXII

Bobby Finds He Has a Neighbor

In his new home in the little cave in the ledge of rocks deep in the Green Forest Bobby Coon at last slept peacefully. There was no one to disturb him, and so he made up for all the time he had lost. He slept all the rest of that day, and when he awoke, jolly, round, red Mr. Sun had gone to bed behind the Purple Hills, and Mistress Moon had taken his place in the sky.

At first, Bobby couldn't think where he was. He rubbed his eyes and stared hard at the stone walls of his bedroom and wondered where he was and how he came to be there. Then, little by little, he remembered all that had happened —how he had made a mistake in thinking he could take Unc' Billy Possum's home away from him; how he had heedlessly crept into Prickly Porky's house for a nap, only to be driven out by Prickly Porky himself; how he had found a splendid hollow stump but had been discovered there by Blacky the Crow and afterwards by Buster Bear; how Buster Bear had chased him and given him a terrible shaking in the top of a slender young tree; how Buster had stopped to chase Peter Rabbit; how he, Bobby, had taken this chance to run until he could run no more and found himself in a strange part of the Green Forest; how he had looked in vain for a hollow tree in which to make a new home, and lastly how he had found this little cave in the ledge of rock. Little by little, all this came back to Bobby, as he lay stretching and yawning.

At last, he scrambled to his feet and began to examine his new house more carefully than he had when he first entered. The more he studied it, the better he liked it. Having no one else to talk to, he talked to himself.

"The first and most important thing to look for in a house is safety," said he. "I used to think a good stout hollow tree was the safest place in the world, but I was mistaken. Men can cut down hollow trees. That is what happened to my old house. But it can't happen here. No, sir, it can't possibly happen here. Neither can Buster Bear tear it open with his great claws. And the entrance is so narrow

Buster Bear wanted to be neighborly. *See page 93*

that no one of whom I need be afraid can possibly get in here. This is the safest place I've ever seen.

"The next most important thing is dryness. A damp house is bad, very bad. It is uncomfortable, and it is bad for the health. This place is perfectly dry. It will be warm in winter and cool in summer. I can't imagine a more comfortable house. The only thing lacking is a good bed, and that I'll soon make. On the whole, I guess the finding of this new house is worth all I went through. Now I think I'll go out and get acquainted with the neighborhood and see if I have got any near neighbors."

So Bobby went out through the narrow entrance and began to look about to see what he could discover. "I think," said he, "that I'll follow this ledge and see if there are any more caves like mine. I might find a better one, though I doubt it."

He shuffled along, light of heart and brimming over with excitement and curiosity. You know it always is great fun to explore a strange place. He had gone but a little way when he came to a sort of big open cave in the rock. Bobby stopped and peered in. Almost the first thing he saw was a bed. It was a big bed, and it was made of dry leaves and little branches of hemlock. It was a very good bed, and it was clear that someone had been sleeping in it very recently. Bobby's eyes grew very round. Then he sniffed.

That one sniff was enough. Bobby turned and ran back to his new house as fast as his legs would take him. All the pleasure he had taken in his new home was gone. He had discovered that his nearest neighbor was none other than Buster Bear himself!

CHAPTER XXIII

Buster Bear Finds Bobby Coon

Bobby Coon was back in his new house, in the little cave in the rocky ledge deep in the Green Forest, and never was he or any member of his family more upset. You see, he had started out in high spirits to see what was to be seen about his new home and to find out who his neighbors might be, and he hadn't much more than started when he discovered that his nearest neighbor was none other than Buster Bear. Wasn't that enough to upset anybody? Anyway, it was enough to upset Bobby Coon, for only a few hours before Buster Bear had tried to catch him and had threatened to eat him. So all desire to spend the night looking about left Bobby the very instant he found Buster Bear's home in that very same rocky ledge in which his own new home was.

"What a dreadful fix, what a dreadful, dreadful fix I'm in," whined Bobby. "Here I've found the best home I've ever had, and now I find that Buster Bear lives almost next door. I don't dare stay here, and I haven't any place to go. Oh, dear, oh, dear, what can a poor little fellow like me do? I wish I were as big as Buster Bear, I do. Then I'd fight him, I would. I'd fight him."

"Whom would you fight?" demanded a great, deep, grumbly, rumbly voice from outside his doorway.

Bobby just dropped right down where he was and shook with fright. But he took great care not to make a sound, not the teeniest, weeniest sound. Perhaps Buster Bear didn't know who it was he had overheard. Perhaps, if he kept perfectly still, Buster would think he had been mistaken.

"Who are you in there, anyway?" demanded the deep, grumbly, rumbly voice. "I didn't know anyone was living here. Why don't you come out and be sociable?"

Bobby simply shivered and kept his tongue still. For a minute or two there was no sound from outside. Then there were three long sniffs—sniff, sniff, sniff! They made Bobby shiver more than ever.

"Oh, ho! So it's you, Bobby Coon! It's my little Cousin Bobby!" exclaimed the deep, grumbly, rumbly voice of

Buster Bear, followed by a chuckle. "Welcome to the old rock ledge, Bobby. Welcome to the old rock ledge. If I am to have such a near neighbor, I'm glad it is to be you. Come out and shake hands. Don't be so bashful. I won't hurt you."

At that Bobby pricked up his ears a little. He knew that Buster's nose had told him all he wanted to know, and that there was no use to pretend any longer.

"Do you really mean that, Cousin Buster?" he asked in a faint voice.

"Certainly I mean it. Of course. Why not? I usually mean what I say," grumbled Buster Bear.

"That's just the trouble," replied Bobby timidly. "Just a little while ago you tried to catch me and said that you would eat me, and I thought you meant it."

Buster Bear began to chuckle and then to laugh, and his laugh was deep and grumbly-rumbly like his voice.

"That's so, Bobby! That's so!" said he. "But that was when my stomach was so empty that it made me lose my temper. Now my stomach is full, and I'm really myself. You know you don't need to be afraid of me when I am

93

myself. Just forget that little affair. I should have, if you hadn't reminded me of it. I'm glad you've decided to be neighborly. You couldn't make your home in a safer place. I'm going to take a nap now. Come over and see me when you feel like it. Be neighborly, Cousin Bobby. Be neighborly."

With this Buster Bear went shuffling along to his own house and bed. As for Bobby Coon, he was soon in the best of spirits again. He decided to remain right there, and he is there this very minute, I suspect, unless he is out getting into mischief or seeking new adventures.